I Win!

Lynne Rickards
Melanie Williamson

Green Bananas

EGMONT

We bring stories to life

First published in Great Britain 2007
by Egmont UK Ltd
239 Kensington High Street, London W8 6SA
Text copyright © Lynne Rickards 2007
Illustrations copyright © Melanie Williamson 2007
The author and illustrator have asserted their moral rights.
ISBN 978 1 4052 2750 6
10 9 8 7 6 5 4 3 2 1
A CIP catalogue record for this title is available from the British Library.
Printed in Singapore.

School Clothes

Saturday Swim

Nana's Visit

for Anna

L.R.

for Heather, thanks for all

your help

M.W.

School Clothes

'Ella! Sam! It's time to get dressed,'
called the twins' mum.

Ella found her grey skirt and pulled
it on.

Then came her white top and
her purple sweatshirt.

'Only the socks left,'

announced Ella.

Sam hated dressing for school. It wasn't easy getting things on the right way.

Ella found one shoe. 'I'm going to
win!' she told Sam.

'I'm not racing,' Sam answered with

a frown.

'Time to get going,' said Mum.

After school, Ella and Sam had a

snack and did their homework.

'Bath's ready!' called Mum from the

bathroom.

Sam raced up the stairs. Clothes

were flying everywhere!

'Off is so much easier!' said Sam.

Mum nodded.

Help!

'Wait for me!' called Ella.

'I win!' shouted Sam with a splash.

I win!

Saturday Swim

The next morning, Dad took the twins swimming.

Ella and Sam raced to get their suits on. They struggled to pull on their armbands.

'No running,' warned Dad. 'You'll slip.'

Careful!

Ella dipped her toe in. 'The water's

nice!' she called.

Ella and Sam jumped in, but Dad
went down the steps. 'I might splash
all the water out of the pool!' he
laughed.

Come on,
Dad!

'Throw me in the air, Dad!'

said Sam.

'Watch me float on my back!'

said Ella.

'One thing at a time,' smiled Dad.

'Let's have a race,' Ella said. 'First one to Dad is the winner.'

'On your marks, get set, GO!' said Dad. Ella and Sam zoomed off.

Both twins were splashing madly

and couldn't see each other.

Crash! Both Ella and Sam reached
Dad at the same moment and
bumped together, coughing and
blinking.

'I win!' spluttered Ella. 'I was first!'

'You were not!' coughed Sam.

'Never mind,' said Dad. 'You both win the After Swimming Prize. A visit from Nana!'

'Hooray!' they said.

Nana's Visit

Ella and Sam couldn't wait to get

home. Nana was coming to stay!

When the doorbell rang, Ella

jumped up. 'I'll get it!' she shouted.

'No, let me!' said Sam, running after

her.

'Hello, my little chickabiddies!'

smiled Nana as the door opened.

'Let your Nana come in!' laughed

Mum.

37

Sam took Nana's hand. 'Come and build a train track with me,' he said.

Ella pulled on Nana's other hand.
'Come and see our new hamster
first.'

'I think what Nana would really like

is a cup of tea,' said Mum.

'I won two races in gym last week!'

said Ella proudly.

40

'My picture of an aeroplane is up
on the wall at school,' added Sam.

Well done,
dear!

'Nana, why don't we do some drawing now?' suggested Sam.

'No, let's play in the garden,'

said Ella.

'I have an idea,' said Nana.

She pulled a big book out of her bag

and led the way to the sitting room.

Nana sat down, and the twins

snuggled up beside her.

'Once upon a time,' read Nana, 'there were two little tigers . . .'

'Which one was the cleverest?'

asked Ella.

'The boy tiger, of course!' said Sam.

Nana shook her head. 'They were both so clever that winning didn't matter.'

'Just like us, then!' joked Ella.

And Nana and the twins laughed

and laughed.